Sarah Somebody

Sarah  Somebody

by

Florence and Louis Slobodkin

NEW YORK · THE VANGUARD PRESS, INC.

Standard Book Number 8149–0663–x
Library of Congress Catalog Card Number 75–103162

Manufactured in the United States of America

FOR SARAH
Who grew up
and became our Mama,
and is now Grandma and
Great-Grandma, too

Contents

Sarah Somebody

Chapter One
The Secret

Sarah sat on the nice flat rock under the big tree and looked down the road. Her little sister, Rachel, played quietly with a rag doll that Grandma had made.

From where she sat Sarah could see only one house until the road curved. And there was not a person in sight . . . not yet. But Sarah knew that soon Grandma would be coming around the bend.

Grandma was very, very old . . . ninety years old! She had lived in Poland all of her ninety years. She said that a long time ago Poland had had a king. Then, she remembered, there were wars. And now, in 1893, Poland was part of another country . . . Russia.

"But," Grandma said, "no matter who rules this land, it does not seem to matter to us in this little village. Most of us have always been poor. That does not change."

Grandma lived half a mile past the bend in the road with Aunt Tessie and her family. Aunt Tessie, like Sarah's Mama, was one of Grandma's many children.

Mama was very busy with her family and her housework. She could not visit Grandma often, and there were no telephones. So Grandma, who was not busy, walked over almost every day to visit Mama, who was her youngest child.

When Grandma came slowly around the turn of the road in the distance she looked even tinier than she was.

"Come, Rachel, let's go to meet Grandma," said Sarah.

Sarah was in full charge of her baby sister and never went anywhere without her. Sarah's two brothers,

Aaron and Samuel, were older than Sarah. They, like other Jewish boys, spent most of their time studying the prayer books, the Bible, and the other Holy Books that teach the Hebrew laws and way of living.

The other children, Miriam, six years old, and Rebecca, three, played together and could now be trusted to stay near the house.

But baby Rachel had to be watched at all times. Often Mama, who seemed to see everything everywhere even when she was working in the kitchen, would come to the door and say, "Bring Rachel back to the front of the house. She must not go near the chickens," or "Rachel is too close to the water barrel."

And Sarah would run to keep Rachel from getting hurt.

Rachel walked very slowly . . . and so did Grandma. It took some time until they met on the dusty road.

"The road gets longer, it seems," said Grandma with her gentle smile. "Let me lean on you, child."

Sarah took Grandma's arm and held on to Rachel with her other hand as they all walked very slowly back toward the house.

"We walk alike . . . the very old and the very young. Think about that, Sarah," said Grandma.

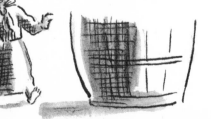

Often when Grandma said something, she would add, "Think about that." And Sarah thought about it and found her Grandma very wise and loved her very much.

When they reached the flat rock under the big tree, Grandma sat down to rest. After a few minutes she said, "Let me hold the baby."

Sarah put Rachel in Grandma's arms but she held on to her.

"She is getting bigger and heavier," said Grandma after a while. "Here, take her."

Then Grandma went into the kitchen to visit with Mama. Rachel tugged at Sarah's skirt.

"All right, I'll walk with you," said Sarah, and she helped the baby walk across the yard and back again to the big tree. "Now, sit here, Rachel, and play with your doll. I'm going into the kitchen for just a few minutes."

Sarah liked to hear Mama and Grandma talk. Every day Grandma brought news of the many cousins and aunts and uncles.

As Sarah came near the door she heard Mama say, "Sh . . . sh . . . Let's not say anything about it in front of Sarah . . . until I've talked with her father. If we cannot do it, I would not want her to be disappointed."

Sarah went into the kitchen. As usual, Grandma was sitting beside the stove. The big brick stove took up almost a whole wall of the kitchen, with just one chair squeezed next to it for Grandma. Even though the weather was warm and there were big, shiny copper pots of food cooking on the stove giving off more warmth, Grandma liked to sit there . . . close to the stove.

There were more chairs in the kitchen and a long table. And there was a cupboard. In this room the family ate, the children played, and the grownups talked.

Standing in the doorway Sarah asked, "What is it that you don't want to tell me, Mama?"

Mama and Grandma looked at each other.

"Tell her," said Grandma. "She's an intelligent child. Even if it cannot be done . . . tell her."

"You've left Rachel alone. Bring her in. And see what Miriam and Rebecca are doing . . . I don't hear them." Mama stopped kneading the noodle dough and wiped her hands on her apron.

Sarah ran out. Miriam and Rebecca were now under the big tree playing house. Sarah picked up Rachel and brought her into the kitchen.

"Now, tell me, Mama . . . please," she said.

"Very well. But I must begin at the beginning. Sit down, Sarah."

Mama, too, sat down at the table and took Rachel into her lap.

"This is very important," thought Sarah, looking at the uncut noodle dough and thinking of all the potatoes

that had yet to be peeled and all the other work from which Mama was taking time.

"You know Mr. Joseph Chesnov and his wife," began Mama. "They visit us sometimes."

Sarah nodded.

"Well, they have an only child, a daughter."

"I didn't know that," said Sarah. "I've never seen her."

"That is so. You have never seen her. Because for more years than you are alive . . . you are now nine years old? . . ." Mama's voice rose to a question.

"Yes," nodded Sarah.

"It must be ten years since Chesnov's daughter left for Warsaw," interrupted Grandma.

"Yes," Mama went on. "Ten years ago she was sent to the big city of Warsaw to live with Mr. Chesnov's rich brother and his wife who have no children of their own. They brought her up and sent her to school. And now she has come back, an educated lady . . . a somebody.

"And," went on Mama, "Miss Chesnov has let it be known that she will take students . . . in her father's house. Grandma has just brought the news."

"But the boys are already studying with Father," said Sarah.

"Yes, and the little sisters are too young," said Mama. "We were thinking of you. . . ."

"Me!" cried Sarah. "But you have said that only boys study . . . with Father or another melamed."

"I said that," said Mama, "because that has been the way in this village. It was thought that men needed to study nothing more than our Hebrew books, and that women did not need to learn to read and write at all."

"That is why, Sarah," interrupted Grandma, "neither your mother nor I nor any other woman in this village was taught to read or write . . . not even to write our names."

"But now we feel the need for learning for girls as well as for boys . . . and for Polish and Russian as well as Hebrew," Mama went on. "In Warsaw, Miss Chesnov went to a school that taught those languages . . . and other things too . . . and taught girls as well as boys!"

"Can anybody go to that wonderful school?" asked Sarah.

"No, child," said Mama. "Such schools cost so much that only the very rich can afford to send their children.

Miss Chesnov's uncle must be very rich indeed to have paid for her in such a school."

"Perhaps someday our government will provide free schools. And perhaps there will even be laws saying that children must go to school," laughed Grandma.

"What a wonderful day that would be," said Mama. "But I can't believe such a thing will ever happen."

Sarah could not hold back her excitement any longer.

"*I* will go to school! And *I* will learn to read the books that Father and the boys read!"

"No, Miss Chesnov will not teach Hebrew. She will teach Polish, the language of this land, which your Father learned without a teacher," said Mama proudly. "And perhaps she will teach other things too. But what is most important is that she will teach reading and writing. A person feels lost who cannot understand some printed word, I can tell you that."

"I, too," said Grandma. "How many times in my life have I wished I could read. And even now, at my great age . . . if only I could write my name . . . I would feel like a somebody!"

Sarah stared at Grandma. Because Grandma was so old, Sarah had never thought there were things that she still wanted . . . things she had never had or known . . . like writing her name.

Sarah felt the tears rush into her eyes. She did not know if she was crying for Grandma or because she was so happy at the thought of school.

"Mama," she managed to say, "you said you must talk to Father. Why wouldn't he want me to go?"

"Because Miss Chesnov wants four gulden a month for every child. Father may feel we cannot spare that much money. You know it is very seldom that he is paid in money for his teaching. Our poor neighbors pay what they can. The shoemaker will give Father a pair of shoes for weeks of teaching his sons. The baker pays with bread. . . ."

Mama sighed and went on. "I will talk with Father tonight. We must decide soon. Many families will want to send their children and there may not be room for all. You know how small the Chesnov house is." Mama turned to Grandma.

"Yes, I know," said Grandma. "And I know, too, that every family—if they have the money—will want to send their children."

Sarah could not bear to hear any more. Besides, Rachel had crawled out of Mama's lap and was moving toward the door. Sarah picked her up and carried her out into the yard. She sat down on the rock with her sister in her arms.

"Did you hear, Rachel?" she asked. "If I go to the school . . . I will learn to read and write . . . to write my name, too! I won't have to make a mark like Mama does. Oh, Rachel, do you know what it means to be able to read and write?"

Rachel did not answer. She wriggled out of Sarah's arms and toddled across the yard.

Chapter Two
Exciting News

That night, as Sarah set the table for supper, she said, "Mama, you won't forget to ask Father . . . about the school, I mean. . ."

"I know what you mean, child," said Mama. "I, too, have thought of nothing else since Grandma told us about it. Yes, I will tell your father as soon as I think the time is right."

Sarah knew what Mama meant by that. The time to tell Father things was not the minute he came home, tired, hungry, and discouraged. Father worked as a melamed. He went to people's houses teaching their sons the Hebrew prayers and the laws of the Hebrew people, just as he taught his own sons at home.

Some of the boys were not interested. Some found learning difficult. Father was a scholar, and when he worked with children who were not interested in learning, it made him very sad.

But after he had eaten the potato soup and the good black bread that he brought home from the baker's in part payment for his lessons to the baker's sons, Father felt better. His sad blue eyes grew brighter; his long, sensitive face with the golden beard seemed to relax.

Tonight Father was in a good mood when he came home. Father was a quiet man and usually when he ate he did not talk. The little he had to say could wait until later.

But tonight Father talked as he ate.

"It's good to be home again," he said, looking around at his bustling wife and his sons and daughters.

"One would think you had been far away," said Mama. "You were only at Saul's, the baker, were you not?"

"Yes, and the youngest son, the one I thought would always be a nobody, is at last beginning to grasp a little knowledge." Father smiled, pleased at his success with the slow-learning boy.

"And," he went on, "speaking of knowledge . . . our Sarah seems to be anxious for learning. I have seen her look longingly at the boys' books. But since she is only a girl, those studies are not for her."

Sarah and Mama stared at him. What had made Father say that—tonight?

"I hear Joseph's daughter who lived with his rich brother in Warsaw is home. She's going to open a school for girls."

"Oh," said Mama, looking at Sarah. So Father had heard too!

"I hear she—Joseph's daughter, that is—wants four gulden a month for each student. Can we afford to send Sarah?" Mama spoke fast, as if she had been holding back the words for a long time.

"I have thought about it all afternoon," said Father, "...since it was mentioned at the baker's. Sarah must go to the school. We'll manage somehow. For one thing, I will ask some of my students' parents to give me a little more money instead of paying mostly with cloth or bread or flour."

Mama smiled at Sarah.

"You see, things have turned out just as we hoped," she whispered.

Sarah was too happy to speak. Her brothers and little sisters looked at her. The brothers who had studied with Father since they were very little did not understand why anyone would be so excited at going to school.

Father said, "Tomorrow, take Sarah to Joseph's house and make the arrangements. We will find a way to pay."

"Yes, tomorrow we will go," said Mama.

Chapter Three
The School

Early the next morning Sarah jumped out of the bed she shared with her two sisters. In the little crib beside her Rachel was already awake and talking to herself.

Sarah brought water into the kitchen from the pump outside and washed and dressed Rachel and herself. Then there was nothing to do but wait.

After a while Mama came into the kitchen and then the others came. Mama looked at Sarah and said, "You are all ready to go? It's too early to call on anyone. So be patient . . . we'll go soon."

"Go where?" asked Sarah's brother Aaron. "And why is Sarah all dressed up in her Sabbath dress?"

"Go where?" repeated Sarah. "Didn't you hear last night? I'm going to school . . . that is, we're going to make arrangements today."

"Oh, I forgot," said her brother.

He forgot! How could anyone forget such a thing, thought Sarah.

Breakfast seemed to take longer than usual that day. But at last it was over. Father and the boys went into the back room to their studies. Miriam and Rebecca went out to play. Mama tied her shawl around her, picked up Rachel, and said, "Now we will go, Sarah. Come."

Sarah walked along beside Mama. Only Rachel chattered her funny baby words. Mama and Sarah were too excited to talk.

When they came to a little gray house just past the bend in the road, Mama said, "There it is. That's the Chesnov house."

Mrs. Chesnov was sitting on the steps in front of the house with a pile of lima beans in her lap and a shiny copper pot beside her. She worked very fast shelling the beans and throwing them into the copper pot.

When she saw her visitors she called out, "Good morning, Hannah. It's been a long time since you've honored me with a visit." Then she smiled and said, "I can guess why you've come. That is your oldest daughter and she is ready for school. But have you heard . . . my educated daughter must get four gulden every month for each student?"

"Yes, I know. And still I have come," said Mama proudly. "So you see that I am prepared to pay the four gulden every month."

"Very well," said Mrs. Chesnov. "My daughter is not at home now. But I will tell her. School begins on Monday at eight o'clock. Send the money with the child."

Then Mrs. Chesnov made a bag of the apron that was tied around her waist and that held the unshelled beans. With one hand she held the apron in front of her and with her other hand she picked up the copper pot.

"Now that we've finished talking about the school," she said, "will you come in and visit for a while?" And without waiting for an answer, Mrs. Chesnov led the way into her house.

Mama put the baby down and said, "Sarah, wait here with Rachel. I won't be long."

Sarah looked longingly after Mama and Mrs. Chesnov. She would have liked to go into the house too, to see where the school would be, but she had not been invited. She sat down on the step left vacant by Mrs. Chesnov and watched Rachel put her doll to sleep.

After some time Mama came out, followed by Mrs. Chesnov, who was holding two cookies. She handed one to Rachel and the other to Sarah.

"May you enjoy your learning," she said.

After they left Mrs. Chesnov, Mama said, "Watch carefully as we go home, Sarah, so that you will know how to come here on Monday."

Sarah smiled. "I won't ever forget the way to this house . . . my school," she said.

Chapter Four
Sarah Becomes a Somebody

Monday came as Mondays have a way of doing, and Sarah dressed hurriedly and ate her breakfast. Mama would take care of Rachel today and would every day when Sarah went to school.

"Miriam is old enough to help me take care of Rachel," Mama had said. "We will get along. Don't worry."

So it was with a light heart that Sarah rushed off to school, running almost all the way. When she came near the Chesnov house she stood still for a few minutes.

Then, very slowly, she walked up the two steps. Her

teacher's father, a big, red-faced man, stood inside the doorway.

"Who are you?" he asked in a loud voice.

"I am Sarah, Bezalel's daughter."

"You are expected," said Mr. Chesnov. "You may give me the money."

Sarah dug into her apron pocket and unpinned the little bag that Grandma had made out of a scrap of gingham.

"This is my present to you. May you enjoy your learning," Grandma had said, and had shown Sarah how to pin the bag into her pocket.

Now Sarah handed the bag to Mr. Chesnov and let him take out the money.

"And be sure you get the bag back," Mama had said.

Sarah had worried. "What if the teacher or whoever collects the money doesn't give it back to me? Will I have to ask for it?"

But Mr. Chesnov did not have to be asked. He counted the money and found there were exactly four gulden, which he put into his pocket. Then he handed the little bag to Sarah, who pinned it back into her apron pocket.

The room was small. It had been emptied of any furniture but a stove in the center and benches and chairs wherever they would fit around the room.

Sarah had heard Papa talk about Mr. Chesnov's stove. A weary peddler had once come by and for a few nights' lodging at the Chesnov's had given them the old stove, which he had in a corner of his wagon.

"I bought it for a few kopecks," the peddler had said. "But it's not the kind of stove anybody here wants. It comes from America."

And near the stove there was one special chair with a red-cushioned seat.

"That's the teacher's chair," thought Sarah.

She chose a seat that was not too close to the teacher's. She did not want to appear greedy by taking a chair right near Miss Chesnov.

There were already two other girls in the room. Sarah did not know them and, even if she had, she would not have spoken. How often had she heard Father complain when he taught a few children at a time, "How can they learn if they talk?"

Very soon more girls came in. Sarah's cousin Naomi was there. She smiled at Sarah but did not speak. Most of the other children Sarah had never seen before. They must have come from great distances to this school, she thought.

Then an elegant lady in a brown dress came into the room.

"Good morning. children," she said, "I am Miss Chesnov."

The children did not answer. Even if she had wanted to, Sarah could not speak for the lump in her throat.

"When I say 'Good morning,' you must answer. You, too, must say, 'Good morning,'" said the teacher.

That was the first thing Sarah learned in school. Every day after that, when Miss Chesnov said, "Good morning, children," the children answered, "Good morning, Miss Chesnov."

Sarah learned many other things. Miss Chesnov taught the Polish language and arithmetic. There were no printed books and no blackboards. The teacher went from pupil to pupil, writing in each child's notebook.

Every day after school Sarah came home with some new words learned. She would write them at home again and again. In her excitement she wanted to share her learning with her family.

"See, this word means 'house,'" she would say, showing her notebook. "And this is the word for 'book.'"

But after a while Sarah quietly studied by herself at home and learned whatever she could in school.

Two of the older children in the class had learned to write a little before they came to the school. They were seated together and were called the advanced group.

Sarah started in the beginners' group but was soon ahead of the other children there.

One day she asked Miss Chesnov if she could join the advanced group.

"Not yet, Sarah," said the teacher. "It is true you learn quickly and are ahead of many of the other beginners, but you are not ready for the advanced group."

"I can write my name," said Sarah.

"I know. You write your name very nicely," Miss Chesnov smiled. "But that is not enough. What else can you do?"

"I can write the name of everyone here."

"You can?" The teacher sounded doubtful. "If that is so, you should be in the advanced group."

"Please," said Sarah, "may I show you?"

Miss Chesnov wrinkled her brow.

"Yes," she said. "Write the names of all the girls in the class . . . if you can."

The teacher turned to the class.

"Let us go back to work, children, while Sarah writes."

Sarah sat down and on a clean page in her book wrote first her own name, then the name of her cousin Naomi, then other names. After a while she looked up to see which children she had missed. And she wrote their names. Then she counted the names in her book and the children sitting in the class.

She had them all . . . eighteen names.

The other children kept looking up from their books to steal glances at Sarah. Even the teacher, although she moved from child to child and bent over each notebook and wrote in it, often looked Sarah's way.

When Sarah stopped writing, the teacher asked, "What is it? Do you need help with any of the names?"

"No, Miss Chesnov, I have written eighteen names," said Sarah.

Miss Chesnov walked over to Sarah and took her notebook.

She read aloud, "Sarah . . . very good. You do have an exceptionally beautiful handwriting. . . . Naomi, you have written her name correctly too . . . and Judith . . . and Deborah."

The teacher read the other names to herself. Then she said, "Children, Sarah has written every name correctly . . . and beautifully. There is no doubt in my mind now. Sarah belongs in the advanced group."

"Hurray for Sarah!" cried Deborah, clapping her hands.

Miss Chesnov took up the applause and the others applauded after her. They all clapped for Sarah!

Above the noise Naomi tried to make herself heard. She tried to tell everyone, "Sarah is my cousin, you know. . . ."

That day Sarah ran almost all the way home. As soon as she came into the house, Mama and Grandma asked, "What is it? What has happened?"

Sarah stared and said, "How did you . . . ?"

Mama laughed.

"You wonder that we know something has happened? Look at yourself in the mirror, child. I have never seen you so excited."

When Sarah had told the good news, Grandma said, "Tomorrow I will not come here. I will go to visit my daughter Regina and her family and tell them that Sarah is now a somebody!"

Later, Father and Sarah's brothers heard about her

promotion. Father smiled and all evening he hummed a little tune, as he always did when he was happy.

The next day was Friday, so there was no school. On Fridays everyone in the village prepared for the Sabbath. Girls helped their mothers scrub the floors and shine the copper pots. The brass candlesticks that held the candles over which the mothers said the Sabbath Eve prayers were polished till they shone like gold.

And on Fridays there was much cooking and baking to be done before sundown. For there was no work of any kind on the Sabbath, not even cooking; enough food was prepared on Friday to feed the family for two days.

After the house was cleaned and the food cooked, everyone bathed and put on Sabbath clothing. At sundown the men and boys went to synagogue and when they returned, the family sat down to supper. It was then, before the meal, that Mama said the prayer over the Sabbath candles in the shiny candlesticks.

During the week the people, who were poor, ate simply—a noodle pudding, boiled carrots, potato soup, or any other food that could be cooked out of what grew in their little gardens or that was given them in exchange for something they gave or did for their neighbors.

But Friday was different. On Friday night there was gefüllte fish and chicken soup with noodles and boiled chicken, and other delicious foods. The food was so delicious and everyone was always so hungry that there was never enough to satisfy the children's appetites.

Sometimes Mama said, "Perhaps someday we will be rich enough to cook more chickens for one meal . . . and to buy more fish . . . and everyone will have as much as he wants of everything!"

Sarah found it hard to believe that she would ever have enough fish and chicken to eat, or that she would ever not be just a little hungry all the time.

But Friday was a happy time just the same.

Saturday, the Sabbath, was another special day. It was the one day in the week when Mama was not busy. Wearing her Sabbath wig, she sat in the yard and waited for her neighbors, who walked over to chat.

Sarah always loved the Sabbath. But this week she was happy when Sunday, a school day, came again and she joined her new group at school.

Chapter Five
Mama Sews a Dress

On the first day of every month Mr. Chesnov waited at the door for the children to pay their four gulden. If a child came without the money and said, "Oh, I forgot to ask my father. I forgot it was the first of the month again," Mr. Chesnov would frown darkly.

"Does my educated daughter forget to come here to teach you? Be sure to bring it tomorrow."

And if the child came the next day and whispered, "My father does not have the money. He says he will have it tomorrow surely," Mr. Chesnov said, "Tomorrow then, without fail. Remember! Everyone must pay!"

Sarah always had the money ready in her little bag. Father always remembered, "Tomorrow is the first of the month. Here are four gulden for Sarah's school."

But one day near the beginning of the month when Sarah came home from school, Mama said, "Sarah, take care of Rachel. And keep an eye on Miriam and Rebecca. I must go to see Mr. Chesnov."

"My teacher's father?" asked Sarah. "Is it about me?"

"Yes, child," said Mama. "I must explain to him that we can't pay the four gulden this month . . . not this week, at least. . . . Perhaps we will have it next week."

"But Mr. Chesnov says he can't wait for the money . . . ever," cried Sarah.

"Don't worry. It will be all right," said Mama as she left.

But Sarah did worry.

What if Mr. Chesnov said, "If you can't pay, take

Sarah out of school this month"? Or what if he said, "If you can't pay, take Sarah out of school forever. We have another child who can pay to take her place"? Or what if . . . what if . . . what if . . . ?

Sarah was most unhappy for the next hour. When her sisters spoke to her she did not answer. Feeling that something was wrong, Rachel crept into Sarah's lap and kissed her.

Sarah burst into tears and, seeing their big sister cry, the other children began to cry too.

And that was how Mama found them when she came home.

"What has happened?" cried Mama. "Is anything wrong?"

"Sarah is crying," said Rebecca, as if that explained her own tears.

"Mr. Chesnov," said Sarah, "what did he say?"

"Oh, you silly girl," laughed Mama, "so that's what it is. Well, I told you there was nothing to worry about. It's all settled. I'm going to sew a dress for Miss Chesnov instead of paying the four gulden for this month."

"Out of the black satin?" guessed Sarah, forgetting her tears.

"Yes," said Mama. "I told her about the black satin that Uncle sent us from St. Petersburg. It has been lying in my drawer these two years. But there is enough only for a skirt. Miss Chesnov will get material for a top for the dress. I have her measurements already and I'll cut the skirt tomorrow."

"Oh, I'm so happy." Sarah ran to hug her mother.

"There, there, child, it's all right," said Mama. "Come, now, all of you. You too, Rachel. . . . It's time to get ready for supper."

The next day when Sarah met Mr. Chesnov at the school door he did not hold out his hand for the money. Instead, he said, "Go right in."

And a few days later Mama took her sewing basket and the black satin that she had cut into a skirt and went to Miss Chesnov's house. There she fitted it on the teacher and pinned it in many places. Then she brought it home and showed Miss Chesnov's dress to Sarah and the little sisters and Grandma.

"Oh, how beautiful!" gasped the children.

There was now a gleaming white top to the shiny black skirt. Miss Chesnov had given Mama the white material for the dress top.

"I have never seen anything so nice," said Miriam, reaching out to touch the dress.

"Be careful . . . it's full of pins," said Mama, just as Miriam cried, "Ouch, a pin!"

"She had to find out for herself," said Grandma. "Beautiful things are often full of pins. . . . Think about that, children."

A few weeks later the dress was finished. When Miss Chesnov wore it to school there were cries of, "Oh, what a beautiful dress!"

Later, the children tried to guess why Miss Chesnov wore so lovely a dress on an ordinary school day. It was Deborah who had an explanation. She had heard that a young man from Warsaw might be coming to visit Miss Chesnov one day. Perhaps this was the day!

Chapter Six
Names for Sale

The months went by and the weather grew cool. The children now wore sweaters or jackets in class. Miss Chesnov wore a navy blue suit that came directly from Warsaw, Deborah said.

Then suddenly winter came. The wind howled and the frost nipped Sarah's fingers. Miss Chesnov lit a fire in the stove in the middle of the room.

She put in bits of wood and bricks of dried turf. The fire burned slowly but gave off a pleasant warmth. After a while the children sitting close to the fire would feel too warm and take off their sweaters, while those at the outer edge of the circle got less of the fire's warmth and still felt the chill in the air.

One very cold day the fire did not burn well. Miss Chesnov went to call her father.

Mr. Chesnov looked at the fire and said, "There is nothing wrong. You are not using enough turf. More turf will make a bigger blaze and the room will be warm."

Then he turned to the children.

"Tell your parents that during the winter you must bring two kopecks every Monday. That will pay for the turf we must buy to keep you warm. Now, don't forget. I will be at the door on Monday morning to collect the two kopecks."

Another two kopecks a week!

"That makes eight more kopecks a month," groaned Mama. "Well, we will manage."

Sarah sighed with relief. How she would have hated to meet Mr. Chesnov at the door on Monday and have

to say, "I do not have the two kopecks for the turf."

But there was one child who had to do just that.

Luba was a stout, sad-faced girl. On Monday Luba was stopped at the door.

"Where are your two kopecks?" asked Mr. Chesnov.

Luba did not answer.

"You do not have the money?" asked Mr. Chesnov.

"No," whispered Luba.

"When will you bring it?"

"I don't know."

Mr. Chesnov pulled at his beard thoughtfully.

"Well," he said, "you have paid four gulden, so you may come in. But you have not paid for the warmth in this room. Where do you sit?"

Luba pointed to the bench in front of Sarah.

"That is a warm bench," said Mr. Chesnov. "That is for a child who pays for the turf. Here is where you will sit now."

Mr. Chesnov pulled a chair to the outskirts of the room, as far as possible from the stove.

"Sit here," he said.

Fortunately, it was early in the morning. None of the other children except Sarah had arrived. Sarah was too embarrassed for Luba to look at her, and later, all through the lessons, she thought of Luba sitting far from the stove.

Every morning at ten o'clock Miss Chesnov went to the back room for a glass of tea while the children stayed in the classroom. That was their recess.

One day Naomi brought a notebook to Sarah.

"Will you write my name in my brand new book?" she asked. "Your handwriting is so beautiful . . . even Miss Chesnov says so."

"Of course," said Sarah, and wrote "Naomi" in her cousin's book.

"Now write my name," said Deborah, holding out her book.

Sarah started to say, "Of course," when she noticed that Luba had left her seat in the far corner of the room and was warming herself at the fire. As soon as Miss Chesnov returned she would go quickly back to her place in the cold.

"Will you write my name, Sarah?" asked Deborah again.

Deborah was the daughter of the only rich man in the village.

"She can bring two kopecks every week without any trouble, while poor Luba . . ." thought Sarah.

Suddenly she had an idea.

"Deborah," she said, "I will write your name very carefully and very beautifully . . . if you will pay me a kopeck."

Deborah laughed. "One kopeck! Well, that's a bargain. Write my name and here is a kopeck waiting for you."

She took the coin out of her apron pocket and showed it.

Sarah began to write. Since she was to be paid for it, she wrote especially carefully. Deborah was pleased and paid the kopeck.

"I have a kopeck. Write my name," said Judith.
"Write mine, too," said Leah, and then Esther.

By the time Miss Chesnov came back, Sarah had earned four kopecks!

"What are you going to do with all that money?" whispered Naomi.

Sarah put the four kopecks into her little bag and pinned it inside her apron pocket, and just smiled.

When school was over that day Sarah whispered to Luba, "Here are four kopecks. Tomorrow give two of them to Mr. Chesnov and keep the other two for next week."

"They're yours. I don't want them," protested Luba.

But Sarah pressed the coins into her hand.

"Maybe I'll earn some more the same way," she said. "Take them."

Luba shivered a little and took the money.

For the next two weeks she sat near the fire. And although there were weeks after that when Luba could not pay the two kopecks (because Sarah had not been asked to write anyone's name) there were many weeks when Sarah was able to give Luba the money to pay for a seat near the fire.

Chapter Seven
The Last Visit

In the winter Grandma did not come to visit. But in the spring she came again. Every day she walked from Aunt Tessie's house . . . very, very slowly.

One day Grandma said, "Sarah, can you write my name? I would like to see how my name looks in writing."

Mama answered for Sarah. "Sarah can write any name," she said proudly.

"Then write, Sarah," said Grandma. "Write my name."

Sarah got her notebook and sat down. She raised her pencil to write. . . . Then she stopped short.

What was Grandma's name? Sarah had forgotten it.

Sarah had never heard her called anything but Grandma or Mother. Even people who were not related to her called her Grandmother. When Grandma was a little girl she was called by a name like Sarah or Rachel or Naomi. And once Mama had told Sarah what that name was. But Sarah had forgotten.

Sarah looked at Grandma, then at Mama.

Grandma was very wise and she understood.

"The child doesn't remember my name," she said. "It is good that we find that out now. My name is Ruth. And someday when I am gone and you have a daughter, perhaps you will name her Ruth after your Grandma."

"May you live to be a hundred . . . I mean a hundred and twenty," said Mama.

Grandma smiled. "One hundred I have already almost reached. And a hundred and twenty would be too much. So . . . Sarah, you know my name. Now write it."

Sarah wrote in her notebook.

"Here it is, Grandma," she said.

Grandma looked at the writing for a long time.

"So that's how it looks," she said. "Sarah, tear out the page and give it to me."

Sarah tore the page neatly out of her notebook and gave it to Grandma.

"Thank you. Thank you very much. You are a good child," said Grandma.

Then Grandma did something unusual. She kissed Sarah, then she kissed Mama, and then Rachel. And when Miriam and Rebecca came running into the kitchen, Grandma kissed them too.

After she left, Mama said, "Grandma must be very happy."

The next day Grandma did not come. Instead, Aunt Tessie's son Benjamin came to say that early that morning Grandma had fallen asleep in her chair, never to awaken.

Nobody spoke for a few minutes. Then Mama wiped the tears from her eyes and said, "Grandma must have known her time had come. That's why she kissed us good-by. When a person gets to be over ninety years old there are many things she knows. We will miss Grandma very, very much. But after a while we will not cry. Remember that Grandma lived long and happily and died of old age."

Cousin Benjamin said, "Grandma had a piece of paper in her hand when she died. The Rabbi says the name Ruth was written on it in Polish in beautiful handwriting . . . the writing of a somebody. Ruth was Grandma's name. I never knew that. Did you, Sarah?"

"Yes," said Sarah. "I knew."

The End.

j FICTION   A93021

Slobodkin, Florence.
   Sarah Somebody, by Florence and Louis Slobodkin.
New York, Vanguard Press [1970, °1969]

   71 p. illus. 23 cm. 3.95

   A poor little Polish girl learns to write names and becomes some-
one special to her family and school friends.

   [1. School stories. 2. Poland—Fiction]   i. Slobodkin, Louis,
1003   joint author. ii. Title.

PZ7.S6332Sar 3   [Fic]   75–103162
                                      MARC

Library of Congress   70 [4]   A C